Our Emotions and Behavior

Why Should I?

Sue Graves

**Illustrated by Emanuela Carletti
and Desideria Guicciardini**

free spirit
PUBLISHING®

Arin didn't look after **anything**.
He didn't look after his toys.
He broke them all the time.

"You need to **respect** your toys," said Dad.

Arin didn't look after his clothes.
He **never bothered** to hang them
up or put them away in the right places.

"You need to respect your clothes," said Mom.

If anyone asked him to be more respectful, he just muttered,

"Why should I?"

Arin didn't respect other people's belongings either. When he wanted to play with Anish's pirate ship, he just **took it**. He didn't ask first. Even worse, he broke the sails on it.

Anish was upset.

He said Arin should show more respect for **other people's things.**

Later, Arin wanted to borrow a book from Vanna. He ignored the "Do Not Enter" sign on her door. He just **walked in**.

Vanna was angry. She said
Arin should show more respect for
other people's space!

At school, Arin saw his best friend Junior. Junior told him that he was going to watch his first skateboard competition. He was **very excited**.

But Arin laughed at him and said skateboarding was silly.

Junior was upset. He said Arin was **being rude**. He said Arin should respect other people's opinions and not laugh at them!

At recess Arin played with his ball. But he kept kicking it into the class garden. The ball knocked over everyone's pots. The plants spilled everywhere. **Everyone was mad** at him. They told Mr. Counter.

Mr. Counter said Arin should
think about his behavior
when he got home.

Arin was upset. He **didn't mean** to make people mad. He especially **didn't mean** to make Junior sad. He went to talk to Grandma.

13

Arin asked Grandma why people were angry and sad. Grandma said people wanted to be treated respectfully. Grandma asked Arin **how he would feel** if someone broke his toys or laughed at things he liked.

Arin thought about it. He said he wouldn't like it at all! **He was sorry** he hadn't treated people the way he would like to be treated. He said he would **try hard** to be more respectful.

The next day, Arin played more carefully with his toys. He hung up his clothes.

Arin asked Anish **first** if he could play with his racing car.

He knocked on Vanna's door **first** before going into her room.

He said **SORRY** to Junior for not respecting his opinions. He **listened politely** while Junior told the class about the skateboarding competition. He said it sounded like a lot of fun.

Then Arin said **SORRY** to everyone in the class for knocking over their plants. He helped them plant them again. Everyone **was pleased** with Arin for being more respectful.

Arin noticed that everyone **treated him better** because he showed more respect. Being respectful was much nicer!

Can you tell the story of what happens when Ellie throws her ball against her neighbor's wall?

How do you think her neighbor felt in the second picture? How does Ellie feel at the end?

A note about sharing this book

The **Our Emotions and Behavior** series has been developed to provide a starting point for further discussion about children's feelings and behavior, both in relation to themselves and to other people.

Why Should I?
This book looks in a reassuring way at why it is important to have respect, not only for ourselves and our own things but for other people and their possessions, space, and ideas.

The book aims to encourage children to have a developing awareness of behavioral expectations in different settings. It also invites children to begin to consider the consequences of their words and actions for themselves and others.

Picture story
The picture story on pages 22 and 23 provides an opportunity for speaking and listening. Children are encouraged to tell the story illustrated in the panels: Ellie is throwing her ball against her neighbor's wall and making dirty marks. When the neighbor talks to her about it, Ellie stops and cleans the wall. She ends up playing ball with her neighbor's son.

How to use the book
The book is designed for adults to share with either an individual child or a group of children, and as a starting point for discussion.

The book also provides visual support and repeated words and phrases to build confidence in children who are starting to read on their own.

Before reading the story
Choose a time to read when you and the children are relaxed and have time to share the story.

Spend time looking at the illustrations and talk about what the book may be about before reading it together.

24

After reading, talk about the book with the children

- What was the book about? Have the children ever been careless with toys or their clothes? What were the consequences if they did not look after their things? Invite children to talk about their experiences.

- Have they ever experienced someone not respecting them or their possessions? How did that feel?

- As a group, talk about why it is important for people to treat others as they themselves would wish to be treated. Encourage children to take turns speaking and to listen politely while others are talking.

- Look at the picture story and talk about what is shown. Invite children to act out the situation in the picture story. Discuss performances afterward as a group.

- Talk about being part of a school community. Why is it important to show respect for others in school? What examples can children give? Examples may be standing patiently and quietly in a line; not interrupting when others are speaking; not pushing past others; asking first if you want to borrow something; being careful with other people's possessions; and being respectful of other people's opinions. Make a list of these examples and display them in your space.

25

To Isabelle, William A., George, William G., Max, Emily, Leo, Caspar, Felix, and Phoebe—S.G.

Published in North America by Free Spirit Publishing Inc., Minneapolis, Minnesota, 2019

Library of Congress Cataloging-in-Publication Data
Names: Graves, Sue, 1950– author. | Carletti, Emanuela, illustrator. | Guicciardini, Desideria, illustrator.
Title: Why should I? / Sue Graves ; illustrated by Emanuela Carletti and Desideria Guicciardini.
Description: Minneapolis : Free Spirit Publishing Inc., [2019] | Series: Our emotions and behavior | Audience: Age: 4–8.
Identifiers: LCCN 2018020689 | ISBN 9781631984129 (hardcover) | ISBN 1631984128 (hardcover)
Subjects: LCSH: Respect—Juvenile literature.
Classification: LCC BJ1533.R4 G73 2019 | DDC 179/.9—dc23 LC record available at https://lccn.loc.gov/2018020689

Reading Level Grade 2; Interest Level Ages 4–8 ; Fountas & Pinnell Guided Reading Level L

10 9 8 7 6 5 4 3 2 1
Printed in China
H13771018

Free Spirit Publishing Inc.
6325 Sandburg Road, Suite 100
Minneapolis, MN 55427-3674
(612) 338-2068
help4kids@freespirit.com
www.freespirit.com

First published in 2019 by Franklin Watts, an imprint of Hachette Children's Books • London, UK, and Sydney, Australia

Text © The Watts Publishing Group 2019
Illustrations © Emanuela Carletti and Desideria Guicciardini 2019

The rights of Sue Graves to be identified as the author and Emanuela Carletti and Desideria Guicciardini as the illustrators of this Work have been asserted in accordance with the Copyright, Designs and Patents Act, 1988.

Editor: Jackie Hamley
Designer: Peter Scoulding